Not-So-Impossible Tales

Oliver and the Seawigs

Cakes in Space

Pugs of the Frozen North

Arrooooo!

PuGS
OF THE
FRoZeN NoRtH

BY PHILIP REEVE
AND
SARAH McINTYRE

RANDOM HOUSE 🏠 NEW YORK

Text copyright © 2015 by Philip Reeve
Cover art and interior illustrations copyright © 2015 by Sarah McIntyre

All rights reserved. Published in the United States by Random House Children's Books, a division of Penguin Random House LLC, New York. Originally published in hardcover by Oxford University Press, Oxford, in 2015.

Random House and the colophon are registered trademarks of Penguin Random House LLC.

Visit us on the Web!
randomhousekids.com

Educators and librarians, for a variety of teaching tools, visit us at
RHTeachersLibrarians.com

Library of Congress Cataloging-in-Publication Data
Reeve, Philip, author.
Pugs of the frozen north / by Philip Reeve and Sarah McIntyre.—
First American edition.
p. cm—(Not-so-impossible tales)
"Originally published in hardcover by Oxford University Press, Oxford, in 2015."
Summary: New friends Sika and Shen try to beat the odds and win the Great Northern Race—in a sled pulled by a team of sixty-six pugs—in hopes of meeting the Snowfather and having him grant their wish.
ISBN 978-0-385-38796-5 (trade)—ISBN 978-0-385-38798-9 (ebook)
[1. Adventure and adventurers—Fiction. 2. Sled dog racing—Fiction.
3. Pug—Fiction. 4. Dogs—Fiction. 5. Magic—Fiction. 6. Arctic regions—
Fiction.] I. McIntyre, Sarah, illustrator. II. Title.
PZ7.R25576Pug 2016
[Fic]—dc23 2014044369

MANUFACTURED IN CHINA
10 9 8 7 6 5 4 3 2 1
First American Edition

For Dulcie and Laurence

ONE

Winter came in the night, like a white sheet laid over the world. It came so coldly and so fast that the waves of the ocean froze as they rolled. The good ship *Lucky Star* froze with them, trapped tight in the suddenly solid sea.

Shen, the cabin boy, the youngest member of the crew, stirred in his sleep as the sounds of rippling and splashing faded into frozen silence. He snuggled deeper under the covers, trying to keep warm. Into the silence came other noises. First, the creaking of timber as the ice tightened its grip upon the old ship's sides. Then the voice of Captain Jeggings, bellowing, "All hands on deck!"

The crew bumbled blinking from their bunks. Able Seaman Bo; Mungbean, the ship's cook; and Shen. They stumbled out on deck and stared at the frozen waves, which reared up all around them.

"Don't just stand there!" shouted Captain Jeggings, hauling an icy rope. "Get us out of here!"

The rope snapped in his hands with a sound like breaking glass. The *Lucky Star* groaned and quivered as the ice clenched tighter.

"What will we do?" asked Shen.

But Captain Jeggings didn't know. Neither did Able Seaman Bo. Neither did Mungbean. They'd weathered storms and sat out still waters, but they'd never seen a sea like this before.

Creak. Crunch. Big tusks of ice pushed

the planks apart and pierced the *Lucky Star*'s sides. *Slosh*. *Gurgle*. Cold black water that hadn't frozen yet came swirling in. The ship sagged, and all the icicles that decked her rigging tinkled cheerfully. But Captain Jeggings couldn't see anything to be cheerful about.

"The cargo!" he shouted. "We must save the cargo!"

All summer long, the *Lucky Star* had been cruising from port to port, selling this and buying that. Two thousand chunky-knit sweaters from the Isles of Aran, a second-hand snowmobile . . . and sixty-six pugs. Captain Jeggings had said those tiny dogs would sell like hot pies. Now, down in the leaking hold, they let out a terrible howling as cold sea sloshed round their paws.

"The dogs!" shouted Shen. "We must save the dogs!"

Mungbean and Bo went running down the steep stairway that led to the cargo holds and came struggling back up with crates of sweaters. Captain Jeggings hauled the snowmobile over the ship's side. Meanwhile, Shen turned over the boxes where more pugs were sleeping. The tiny dogs raced up on deck and jumped off the *Lucky Star*'s sides onto the ice.

Shen had heard people talk about rats leaving a sinking ship before, but he'd never heard of pugs leaving a freezing one. *There's a first time for everything*, he thought. He

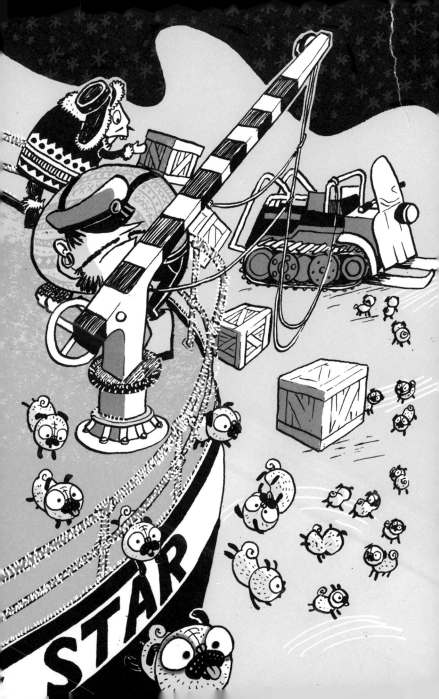

dragged the sack that held their leashes and harnesses up onto the deck and threw it after them.

The *Lucky Star* shuddered again, squeezed in the teeth of the ice. Planks popped out of the deck. The mast trembled like a chopped tree. Captain Jeggings shouted as he jumped over the side.

But Shen had thought of something else that needed to be saved. "The dog food! It's still on board!"

"It'll have to stay there, then!" yelled Bo, jumping down onto the ice with Mungbean. Shen passed the smallest of the pugs down to them, then jumped after them.

With a final heave, the ice crushed the old ship flat.

Shen and the pugs stood and shivered, while Captain Jeggings and the others got the snowmobile ready. Its engine coughed and snarled as they started it up. Into its trailer they piled the crates of cargo—but there was no room for the dogs.

"We can't leave them behind!" wailed Shen.

"Well, we can't stay here with them," said Captain Jeggings. "This ice might melt as quickly as it came, and then where would we be? Way out at sea without a ship under us.

Awkward!" (He had told Shen that the sixty-six pugs would sell like hot pies, but he meant that they would sell *in* hot pies—his aunt ran a pie shop at home, and she was always looking for new ingredients. They were by far the least valuable bit of his cargo, so he had decided to leave them behind.)

"Maybe they'll follow us!" said Shen. He climbed aboard the snowmobile with Bo and Mungbean and the captain. "Come on, doggies!" he called to the pugs.

The dogs looked up at him, heads to one side. Their hot breath steamed and smoldered

in the cold air like the breath of sixty-six tiny dragons.

The snowmobile set off with a roar. The tower of crates in its trailer teetered and swayed as the snowmobile weaved its way between the frozen waves.

The pugs sat where they were and watched it go.

"Come on!" shouted Shen. But they didn't seem to understand.

"Wait for me, Captain!" he yelled, and jumped down off the snowmobile. The frozen waves were slipperier than hills of glass. He slithered over them, back to where the pugs sat, and when they saw Shen coming, their tails began to wag and they ran to meet him.

"Come on, doggies!" he said, patting sixty-six small round heads and getting licked by sixty-six small rough tongues. "You've got to follow Captain Jeggings. . . ."

But when he turned to look for the snowmobile, it was nowhere to be seen. Either Captain Jeggings hadn't heard when Shen shouted for him to wait . . . or he had decided that Shen and sixty-six pugs weren't worth waiting for.

TWO

Shen could still hear the snowmobile's engine buzzing like a distant bee. He started after it, following the scratch marks that its tracks had left along the troughs between the waves. The pugs seemed to understand now that they were meant to come with him, and they did. But they weren't used to walking on ice. Their claws skittered and scrabbled at the frozen sea. They lost their footing and fell on their faces, or slid on their tummies down the steep sides of the stilled waves.

"This is hopeless!" said Shen as he slithered to and fro, trying to help them. The sound of the engine was growing fainter and fainter in the distance. Soon Shen could not hear it at all. He kept following the snow-mobile's tracks while the pugs skidded after him. Big, feathery flakes of snow began to fall. It made the pugs sneeze and covered the tracks completely.

Through the snowflakes, Shen saw something on the ice ahead. It was one of the crates from the snowmobile trailer. It had burst open, and a pile of woolly sweaters had spilled out. Shen guessed it hadn't fallen off the trailer by accident. Bo and Mungbean had always been kind to him, ever since they'd found him as a baby, floating in an upturned umbrella in the South China Sea. They must have tried to persuade Captain Jeggings to stop and wait. When he wouldn't, they'd quietly heaved the sweater crate off the trailer so that at least Shen would have something to keep him warm.

"Thanks, Mungbean," said Shen. "Thanks, Bo."

He put on a couple of the sweaters and looked back. The pugs were trailing after him. They were getting better at walking on the ice, but they were all shivering with the cold, the poor things. Shen took out his pocket-knife. Quickly, he cut the sleeves off thirty-three sweaters and made cozy body stockings for the pugs.

As he was cramming the pugs into the sleeves, he noticed a new sound. *Rummmble*, it went. *Rummmble*.

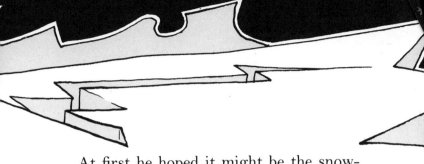

At first he hoped it might be the snow-mobile coming back. . . .

Then he worried that the ice was cracking.

Then he realized that it was the pugs' empty tummies rumbling. No wonder they were going so slowly! They weren't just cold and frightened—they were hungry!

They sat there sadly in their new sweaters, tails down, ears drooping, waiting for their breakfast.

Shen scrambled to the top of a frozen wave and looked around. Through the snow, he saw the dark line of cliffs not far off.

The waves must have hidden it from Captain Jeggings and the others. They would not have seen the lonely lights that twinkled there.

"Wait here!" he told the pugs. "I'm going to get help!"

He spread some of the armless sweaters on the snow, and the pugs piled onto them, snuggling together in a big heap. He laid more sweaters over them and told them that he would soon be back.

Then he set off across the motionless ocean.

THREE

It was hard work walking on that frozen sea. In places the ice creaked alarmingly, and Shen had to back away and find a different route for fear it might not take his weight. In others it was as solid and as clear as thick glass. He brushed away the snow and looked down into cold, gleaming depths, where fish hung imprisoned. Captain Jeggings had been right about one thing: surely there had never been a winter like this before!

As Shen reached the shore, the sun came up, peeking nervously over the edge of the icy world and scattering sequins on the snow. It shone on the frozen fjord that lay between the cliffs. It cast long shadows from the spindly legs of the houses that perched on stilts along the fjord's edge. Smoke was drifting from the houses' tin chimneys. Shen thought they were the coziest, funniest-looking houses he had ever seen. How nice it must be, to live in a house on stilts! He ran up the frozen beach toward the nearest.

A girl no older than Shen was sweeping snow off the front step. Above the door some

letters had been nailed to a wooden plank.
They spelled out a mysterious message:

PO OF ICE

"What's a po of ice?" asked Shen.

The girl looked up. She had a round face,

and her cheeks were rosy with the effort of sweeping. "It's supposed to say post office," she said. "But the *s* and the *t* blew away. Also one of the *f*'s." She tossed her broom aside and held out a small, mittened hand for Shen to shake. "I'm Sika. Who are you?"

"I'm Shen. I've been shipwrecked. Oh, please, I need help and dog food!"

Sika frowned. She had thick black eyebrows like lines drawn with charcoal. They were very good for frowning with. "You have dogs?"

"Yes! They are waiting out on the ice! I have to get them to shore quickly, before the ice melts!"

"Oh, it won't melt!" said Sika. "Don't you know what this is? Didn't you notice how suddenly the cold came? This is no ordinary winter. This is a magical winter. A once-in-a-lifetime winter. My grandpa has told me about winters like this. That ice won't melt till spring. But tell me about your dogs. How many do you have?"

"Sixty-six," said Shen.

"Sixty-six!"

"Yes. So I'm afraid they're going to need a lot of food," said Shen. "And I don't have any money. . . ."

Sika was looking at him, and her eyes sparkled just as brightly as the sunlit snow. "Never mind money! If I give you some dog food, could I have some of your dogs?"

Shen shrugged. He hadn't really thought yet about what he was going to do with the sixty-six pugs. He supposed he couldn't keep them. Not all of them, anyway. And this Po of Ice looked like the sort of place where pugs might be happy. "Yes," he said.

Sika turned and ran inside the Po of Ice. Shen had a glimpse through the door as it closed behind her. It was snug and cluttered

inside, and he saw shelves with tins of soup and racks of tools and big bins labeled OATMEAL and SYRUP. The Po of Ice wasn't just a post office—it was a general store as well, but it didn't look as if it was a very busy one.

"Ma! Grandpa!" he could hear Sika shouting. "I'm going to help a boy who's been shipwrecked! He has dogs! He's going to give us some!"

A moment later she came slamming back out, carrying a bin nearly as big as she was. This one was labeled DOG FOOD.

"Come on," she said. "We'll use Grandpa's sled to get out to your camp on the ice."

Shen helped her carry the dog food bin around the side of the Po of Ice, to a shed.

When Sika booted the door open, the pale snow light shone in and showed Shen a strange shape buried in tarps. As his eyes got used to the dim light, Shen saw that it was a magnificent sled, with sleek whalebone runners.

"I've never seen a sled like that!" he gasped.

"Grandpa built this sled when he was a boy," said Sika. "But we don't have a dog team to pull it anymore. That's why I'm so glad you showed up! Just in time, too! On the first day of True Winter!"

Shen wasn't quite sure what she meant.

"So, if you don't have any dogs to pull it," he said, "how are we going to get it out onto the ice?"

Sika did an eyebrow thing at him, as if to ask, *How stupid are you?*

"We're going to push it, of course!" she said.

FOUR

Up the steep slope behind the Po of Ice they went, puffing and panting, pushing the heavy sled ahead of them. They soon grew hot, despite the cold. Sika pulled off her mittens and hood and let the snowflakes settle in her hair.

But it was all worth it when they reached the top of the headland. From there they could see the pugs out on the ice. The heap of little dogs under their blanket of sweaters looked like a knitted tent.

Shen and Sika climbed onto the sled beside the dog food bin, and Sika pushed off.

The sled went swooshing down the headland's flank. Its runners threw up huge fans of powdery snow as Sika leaned this way and that to steer the sled around the rocks and frozen bushes that loomed in its path.

"Wheeeee!" she shouted.

"Waaaaaargh!" screamed Shen.

The cliffs at the headland's edge were drawing closer.

But Sika knew the headland well, and she had aimed the sled at the place where the cliffs were lowest. They weren't really cliffs at all, more like a stony step, and the sled shot over it, landed with a thump on the sea ice, and kept going, slithering between the frozen waves almost all the way to the camp.

The heap of pugs heard them coming. Sixty-six small dark specks bounced and yapped upon the ice, wagging their tails in welcome.

"There are the dogs!" said Shen.

"Where?" asked Sika, looking around. "Those? Those are *dogs*?"

The pugs had caught the scent of dog food. They crowded around the sled, yipping and whining, wagging their tails. Shen opened the dog food bin and shoveled out scoopfuls of kibble. Soon the yapping was replaced by crunching.

Shen looked around at them happily. Then he looked behind him. Sika was sitting on the sled. She had her head in her hands, and she was crying.

"What's the matter?" he asked.

"Oomph!" went Sika. Tears trickled down her face and dripped off her chin and froze before they hit the ice, where they landed with tiny plinking sounds. "Oomph!" she said. "When you said you had sixty-six dogs, I thought you meant real ones!"

"These *are* real ones!" said Shen.

"No they're not! They couldn't pull a sled!"

"Oh!" said Shen. Now he understood. So *that* was why she had wanted some of his dogs. He looked at the sled—the bigness of it. It needed a team of huskies to tow it, not a team of pugs.

"I thought Grandpa could enter the race after all!" sniffled Sika. "And now I will have to go home and tell him it's hopeless."

"What race?" asked Shen.

"The Great Northern Race," said Sika miserably. "When True Winter comes, the teams arrive from all over the north. They will race through the night forests and across the frozen sea, all the way to the Snowfather's palace at the top of the world."

Shen scratched his head. He remembered the charts he'd seen on board the *Lucky Star*. The North Pole was just a patch of bare paper so big and white it made him want to get a pencil out and draw something, anything, on it. "There isn't any palace at the top of the world," he said.

"There is if it's a True Winter," said Sika. "That's where the Snowfather lives. And he grants the wish of the first adventurer to reach it." She sighed. "Grandpa almost won

it once, when he was not much older than me. Such stories he tells about that journey! And he's waited and waited for True Winter to return ever since. He kept this sled and bred the best team of sled dogs in the north. But True Winter comes only once in a lifetime. The dogs got old and died, and Grandpa got old, too, and soon he'll die. And now True Winter is here at last, and when you said dogs, I thought you meant big dogs; I thought

Grandpa would be able to race after all, and I'd go with him to the North Pole and see the Snowfather. But these are just toy dogs."

"No they're not!" said Shen. "Just because they're tiny, it doesn't mean they're not strong, and loyal, and brave. And I have leashes and little harnesses for all of them. I bet they could pull you and your grandpa all the way to the North Pole easily!"

Sika didn't look as if she believed him, so he ran and got the sack of leashes and harnesses, which was still lying on the ice where the *Lucky Star* had gone down. He started shoving pugs into harnesses and clipping the leashes to the harnesses and knotting the other ends to Sika's sled. (He was very good at knots, having grown up on a ship.)

The pugs caught his excitement and started to yip and yap and dance around, straining and pulling at the heavy thing he'd hitched them to.

Ten pugs couldn't shift the sled at all. Twenty couldn't. Even when thirty were attached, it didn't budge, and Sika said, "See? They just aren't sled dogs. This is hopeless."

But when forty dogs were tied on, the big sled stirred and slid a few inches over the ice. When fifty were attached, it started to gather speed. When the sixty-sixth was in position,

Sika shouted, "Mush, doggies! Mush!" and it shot away as speedily as any normal, husky-powered sled. It whizzed over the frozen waves, throwing up fans of powdered ice each time it turned. The pugs were getting used to running on ice. They kept tumbling over each other and getting their leashes tangled at first, but they soon sorted themselves out, and by the time Sika had circled the pile of sweaters six times, the sled was running straight and true.

She grinned at Shen, her face all rosy with cold and happiness. "It must be the best sled ever! Can I really take your tiny dogs to the North Pole?"

Shen felt a bit unsure about that. He hadn't meant to give her all the pugs. He was going to miss them. But Sika had saved them, and he didn't want to make her cry again, so he said, "All right. . . ."

"I can't wait to tell Grandpa!" she said. And she took a spare leash and cracked it in

the air above the pugs' tiny heads like a whip. Two hundred sixty-four tiny paws pattered on the ice. Sixty-six little voices howled "AROOO!" and the sled set off, back toward the land and the Po of Ice.

FIVE

Once they had made the sled shed into a kennel for the pugs, Shen followed Sika inside. It was cozy in the Po of Ice, warmed by the heat from a busy stove. A woman was heating milk. She had the same charcoal eyebrows as Sika and the same wide smile. "Sika!" she said. "You must be frozen! Did you find your dogs?"

"Yes, Mom!" said Sika.

"And this must be your shipwrecked friend," said Sika's mom. "Poor boy! Is there anyone we can contact for you?"

"Not really," said Shen.

"Well then," said Sika's mother, "I will make a big breakfast for you both."

Sika led him around behind the counter, into a back room, where a big carved bed stood. In the bed, beneath a mound of furs and quilts, lay the biggest man Shen had ever seen. He was so big that at first Shen wasn't even sure he *was* a man; under all those coverings he looked like an old boat that had been brought ashore and turned upside down for winter. Then Shen saw the big gray bearded face resting on the pillows and realized that the rumbling he heard was snores.

"That's Grandpa," whispered Sika.

The old man's face was gray with age, rugged as a mountain rock. Shen remembered Sika saying that her grandpa would soon die and wondered if he was going to do it now. But then beneath one bushy eyebrow, a bright eye opened and turned to stare at Shen.

"Grandpa, this is Shen," Sika said. "He was shipwrecked, and he has dogs with him! We can enter the race!"

"Ah," said the old man. "So Sika has told you about the race?"

"A little," said Shen.

"It did not always used to be a race," said Grandpa in his deep, rumbly voice. "In the olden days, no one knew of the Snowfather or his igloo palace. Then, one True Winter, a brave girl named Ooka strapped on her skis and went exploring. Across Kraken Deep she went, but old Kraken, he was sleeping far beneath the ice and did not trouble her. All the way to the top of the world she went, and when she got there she found the old Snowfather waiting, and he granted her a wish."

Just then, Sika's mom granted Shen's wish, by bringing him a mug of hot chocolate and some hot waffles with honey. Grandpa went on.

"Well, of course, Ooka's story spread far and wide. One lifetime later, when another True Winter turned the sea to ice, all the brave young men of the north went racing off to see if they could get their wishes granted, too. 'Oh no,' said the Snowfather. 'Do you know how hard it is to make wishes come true? Only the one who was first to reach me shall have their wish granted!' And he sent the rest home, disappointed.

"Well, after that, each time True Winter dawned, there were all sorts of fights and rages, everyone trying to be the first to reach the Snowfather. 'We can't have this,' he said, seeing the blood on the snow as young warriors fought each other to be first through the gates of his palace. 'There must be rules! There must be fairness! You must all start together, and the best sled will win.'

"And that is why, ever since, all those who seek the Snowfather's palace set out together,

54

from Snowdovia. That is where I started from, the year I made the trip. . . ."

The wind was rising outside. The thin hissing it made must have sounded to Grandpa like sled runners racing over snow. He closed his eyes and smiled, imagining his bed was a sled, carrying him north.

"Tell us more!" said Sika. "Tell us about Kraken Deep and the *Lost Hope*!"

Grandpa shook his head. "I don't remember those stories anymore," he said. "It was all so long ago. True Winter comes but once in a lifetime, and I have seen two, which means my lifetime must be over. I wish I could see the old Snowfather one more time, but I am too old now to make the journey. My time is nearly done."

"Oh, Grandpa!" said Sika, and Shen thought that she was going to cry again. "Maybe we can take you! You've waited so long!"

"No, Sika," he said. "But you should go."

"Me?" said Sika.

"All on her own?" said Sika's mother worriedly.

"I'll come, too!" said Shen. After all, he thought, it wasn't as if he had anything better to do, now that the *Lucky Star* was wrecked and Captain Jeggings had abandoned him.

"Yes," said Grandpa. "You should both go! You mustn't miss a chance like this! You're young and brave, and the carvings on my sled will keep away the trolls and snowspooks and other creatures that wander abroad in a True Winter. And when you see the Snowfather, say hello from me."

"I'll do better than that," said Sika. "I'll ask him to make you well again, and then you'll remember all the stories and live to see a third True Winter, probably."

"All that way, with only such little dogs to pull you?" said Sika's mother doubtfully. But she had been listening to Grandpa's stories of the Great Northern Race all her life, just like Sika. If she hadn't had to stay and look after him, she would have been jumping on that sled herself.

From outside there came a sound like wild applause. Fireworks were blooming above the frozen hills.

"That is the starting line, down at Snowdovia," said Sika.

Her grandpa reached out and took Shen's and Sika's hands in his. "Good luck!" he whispered. "And now you must go! The race will begin soon!"

SIX

The town of Snowdovia was built in the same style as the Po of Ice, on stilted platforms along a fjord edge. But unlike the Po of Ice, it was full of life and bustle. Bunting and strings of lights festooned the houses. The people of the town lined the balconies outside their homes to watch as the adventurers who meant to race to the top of the world came sledding into their fjord.

From all over the north they came. True Winter had not arrived without warning. Not for people who knew what to look for. Not for people who had been eagerly waiting for the first flake of magical snow to fall. They had

been preparing for weeks, and now that the ice had come, they were ready.

At the Limpetville Institute of Technology, Professor Shackleton Jones had known about the coming winter by the excited way the northern lights made his particle detectors ping. He was determined to reach the top of the world using the power of science. He and his robot companion, SNOBOT, swept into Snowdovia on a carbon-fiber sled so strong and lightweight that it was barely there at all.

On a lonely island not far from Snowdovia, Helga Hammerfest had learned of the big freeze by watching the flight of geese and the way the spiders spun their cobwebs. She had readied her sled and harnessed up her team—no dogs for Helga, just her two pet

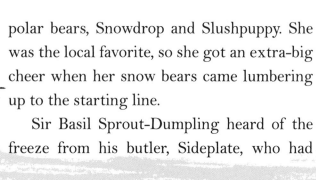

polar bears, Snowdrop and Slushpuppy. She was the local favorite, so she got an extra-big cheer when her snow bears came lumbering up to the starting line.

Sir Basil Sprout-Dumpling heard of the freeze from his butler, Sideplate, who had

been keeping watch on the weather forecasts. Ten minutes later they were at the airport, loading Sir Basil's sled and pedigree dog team aboard an airplane. Sir Basil's father had been the first to reach the top of the world the last time True Winter came. He had met the Snowfather and had his wish granted, which was to be ridiculously rich. He had gone back to England with a fortune in rubies, sapphires, and diamonds, but Sir Basil had spent it all. "If we don't beat these riffraff to the Pole, Sideplate," he said as they drew up to the starting line, "I shall have to sell off the old stately home. I mean to win this race, even if I have to cheat like an absolute slimeball."

"Yes, Sir Basil," said Sideplate sadly, holding his bowler hat on tight and wishing he'd worn warmer underwear. "But if I may say so, Sir Basil, I do hope cheating won't be necessary. . . ."

Sir Basil wasn't listening. "I *say!*" he cried. For the pink sled that had just pulled up next to him held none other than Mitzi von Primm, most glamorous of all the racers. How embarrassed her team of huskies looked, clipped like poodles and dyed pink to match Mitzi's stylish racing outfit!

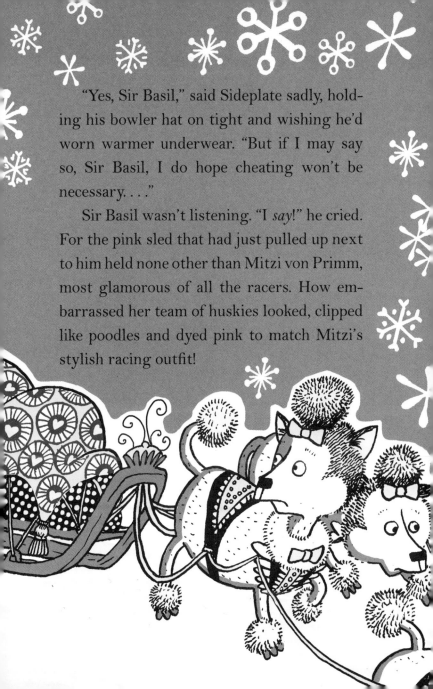

Those four were not the only entrants for the race. There were dozens of others: modern sleds with GPS and central heating, age-old sleds of wood and bone, a sled folded out of stiff paper by an origami master from Japan, and an inflatable sled advertising Poop-B-Gone pooper-scoopers. There was even a sled crewed by two women who were doing the race for charity, dressed in a zebra costume. It took quite a while to get them all sorted out and arranged along the starting line. The overexcited dogs woofed and yapped and howled and sniffed each other's bottoms and started fights. The overexcited race marshals skated to and fro, checking that nobody was cheating and that no dog (or polar bear) had its nose over the line.

They had almost finished, and the Chief Marshal was just cleaning the snow out of her starting pistol and getting ready to fire it, when people standing near the fjord's end began to shout, "Wait! Wait! Here comes another!" A ripple of applause spread along the fjord side as the late arrival headed for the starting line.

"Oh my! That looks like young Sika, in her grandpa's old sled," said the Chief Marshal, scraping away the ice that had formed on the lenses of her binoculars. "But what are those little things pulling it?"

"They look like sixty-six pugs," said her assistant.

"Pugs?" said the Chief Marshal.

"Pugs?" said the other racers, turning to stare as Sika steered the old sled into a gap between Sir Basil's and Mitzi von Primm's and Shen reined in the eager little dogs.

"I say!" complained Sir Basil as the marshals came skating over to take the names of the new arrivals. "They've got sixty-six dogs! That's against all the rules!"

"And it looks like those dogs are wearing

woolly sweaters," agreed Mitzi. "I'm not sure that's allowed."

But Helga Hammerfest, whose sled was on the other side of Mitzi's, said, "Well, dear, your huskies are dyed pink and have ribbons in their fur. I don't think you'll find that mentioned in the rule book, either."

(Mitzi blushed, and her poor pink dogs all hung their heads in shame.)

"And Shackleton Jones's sled is pulled by robot dogs!" Helga pointed out.

"These are Woof-O-Tron 2000s. They're my very latest invention," said Shackleton Jones proudly.

"And those sixty-six little dogs are each about a tenth of the size of one of yours, Sir Basil," Helga went on. "And you've got eight, so you've got more dog power than these youngsters. What's the matter? Afraid that smart sled of yours won't be as fast as their antique?"

"Of course not!" said Sir Basil, but he didn't say it very loudly, because Helga was half as tall as him and twice as wide, and he didn't like the idea of getting into an argument with her. (Also, her polar bears kept giving him very nasty looks.)

So the Chief Marshal wrote Shen's and Sika's names on her clipboard and stepped into the little balloon that was waiting on the fjord side to carry her up above the starting line.

Shen and Sika had left the Po of Ice in a terrible hurry, having quickly packed the sled with supplies for themselves and the pugs. All the way to Snowdovia they had been worrying that they would be too late. Now Sika turned to Shen and beamed. "We did it!"

Shen was not so sure. They were in the race, but that was only the beginning. How could they hope to win it, when the other sleds looked so speedy and the other dogs so big and strong? Still, it would be something just to start. The sound of all the dogs filled the frosty air and made him eager to be off. He waved at Helga and said, "Thank you, sir!"

"She's a lady!" hissed Sika.

"Is she?" asked Shen.

"Yes, I am," said Helga Hammerfest. "But don't worry. I am always getting mistaken for a man, on account of my size, and also beard. Most ladies don't care for beards, but I find that mine keeps my chin warm in the frozen north. You should try growing yours, Miss Mitzi."

Mitzi von Primm shuddered. "My fur-lined racing coat is all I need to keep me warm," she said. "It's by a very good designer, you know—"

The Chief Marshal interrupted, drifting above them in her balloon and shouting through a huge megaphone. Her words boomed across the ice, and broken bits of them came bouncing back from the frozen hillsides.

"Welcome to the Great Northern Race! Now, you all know the course! North, through the Night Forest, then over Kraken Deep, and then by whatever route you want to the palace

at the top of the world. Good luck! Give our
regards to the Snowfather! And may the best
sled win!"

Then she fired her starting pistol. The racers cracked their whips and hollered at their dogs, and the sleds set off, rushing across the ice.

There were some disasters right away, which was only to be expected with so many sleds all starting out together. Some tangled in each other's runners. Some of the dog packs stopped running and started fighting. A speedy Russian sled crashed nose first

into a hole that opened suddenly in the ice. (Sir Basil chuckled and tossed away a can of antifreeze.) A small avalanche, triggered by all the noise, came rushing down the fjord

side and crumpled the origami sled before it had gone ten yards. The inflatable sled popped when one of the dogs pulling the sled behind it mistook it for a huge runaway sausage and took a bite. And three sleds were knocked over when the Chief Marshal's balloon fell on

top of them; she had accidentally punctured it when she fired the starting pistol.

But the others were away. Shackleton Jones was in the lead, with Sir Basil close behind, until Mitzi von Primm took a daring shortcut between two ragged rocks and overtook them both. Helga's polar bears galloped lazily along, not bothering to go too fast yet. And right at the back, pulled by their sixty-six panting pugs, came Shen and Sika.

"It's no good!" shouted Shen, clinging on tight as they left the smooth ice of the fjord and started bounding and bouncing over snowy ground. "They'll be at the top of the world long before us!"

"Maybe not," said Sika. "It's not just about being fast. It's about luck! It will take at least a week to reach the North Pole. All sorts of things will happen on the way! What will you wish for if you get there first?

What's your heart's desire, Shen?"

"I don't know," said Shen. He had been thinking about it a lot as the sled whisked along. He supposed he ought to wish for a family. He had never had one of his own, except for Bo and Mungbean and Captain Jeggings, who didn't really count. But he didn't want a magic family, just an ordinary one. So he said, "I'm still thinking about it."

"I know exactly what I want," said Sika. "I'll ask the Snowfather to make Grandpa well again. To let him live another lifetime, so he'll have a chance to race again next time True Winter comes."

"Can the Snowfather really do that?" wondered Shen.

"Of course he can! He can do anything!"

Shen looked back and wished that he knew what to wish for. He saw that the fjord and the starting line had already fallen far behind.

Zzzzzzzzzssssssssszzzzzzzzsssssss
went the runners, racing over snow and ice.
HoooooOOOOOoOOOoOoOO went the wind,
whistling around the sled's carved stern. And
the sixty-six pugs went . . .

YIP YIP YIP YIP YIP YIP YIP YIP YIP YIP YIP YIP YIP YIP YIP YIP YIP YIP YIP YIP YIP YIP YIP YIP YIP YI

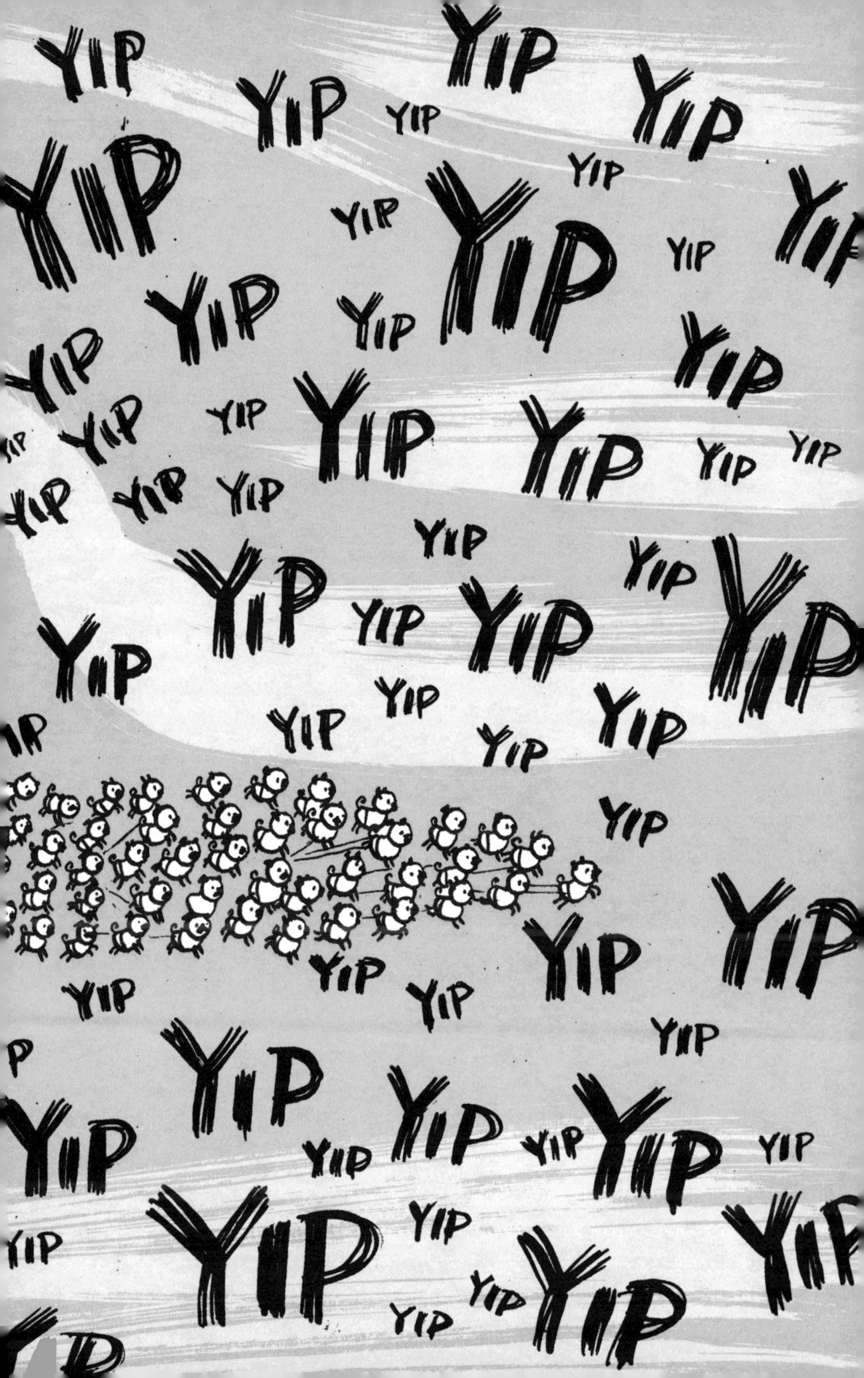

SEVEN

They rushed into the Night Forest, following the tracks of the sleds that had gone ahead of them, weaving between the tall dark trees. Far ahead, they could sometimes hear the deep barking of other sled teams, and the pugs lifted up their little heads and answered: YIP, YIP, YIP! They were loving it. They felt like real dogs at last, the sort of dogs that they were in their secret doggy dreams.

But all that woofing and yipping made the dark trees tremble, and down from the branches slid great dollops of snow—

FLUMP,
FLUMP,
FLUMP.

Somehow, Sika steered her way around the snow without crashing into any tree trunks. Other sleds were not so fortunate. They passed two that had been smashed by the snow flumps, and whose grumpy owners were starting the long walk back to Snowdovia. And near the far edge of the forest they found Shackleton Jones standing under the trees, watching while SNOBOT dug his high-tech sled and robot dog team out of a massive snow dollop. Sika slowed her sled to ask if he needed help, but he just grinned and said, "I have all the help I need! SNOBOT is designed to dig a ton of snow per minute! You'll soon have us out of here, won't you, SNOBOT?" He beamed at the children again. "So, kids! Next stop, Kraken Deep, eh? What's supposed to go on there, do you think?"

"They say the Kraken sleeps there," said Sika. "It's this ancient sea monster with tentacles and things. When True Winter comes, it rises to the surface. If we're lucky, the ice will be thick

enough to stop it from reaching up and grabbing us."

Shackleton Jones laughed. "The Kraken? You don't believe in that old story, do you? It's just a legend of the sea, like the Bermuda Triangle or the Night of the Seawigs."

"Idiot," muttered Sika as they went on. "He'll be saying next that the Snowfather himself is just a legend."

"At least we're not the last anymore!" said Shen, looking back over his shoulder as they left the snow-flumped sled behind. But secretly he was hoping that Shackleton Jones had been right about the Kraken.

They shot out of the forest and went swooshing down a long, smooth slope. They left the land and went speeding over the sea. The ice was smoother here. It was sheltered by high, dark rocks, which poked from the frozen sea in a wide ring. It was as smooth as a skating rink, and all over its surface Shen could see the tracks of the other sleds that had come this way, heading toward the North.

"What a strange place!" he said. "I wonder if the Kraken really does live here."

The frozen sea was as clear as glass—thick and ripply, like the glass in front doors. Shen looked down through it, and from the cold depths, something looked up at him.

The sled was hurtling above an eye the size of a parking garage.

And all those snaky rocks weren't rocks at all—they were the tips of massive tentacles, frozen as the Kraken lifted them up out of the sea.

"Er, Sika?" said Shen.

"What is it?"

Shen looked down at the eye again. He was sure that it was staring right at him. And then, as he stared back at it, it blinked.

Crack! The towering tentacles twitched. Cascades of shattered ice came raining down

their sides like broken glass as the tips waved, trying to break free and snatch Shen and Sika. Cracks spread across the ice.

"Go faster!" Shen shouted.

But the sixty-six pugs were already running as fast as they could. Their little pink tongues were hanging out, and their hot breath made plumes of steam in the icy air. Their paws skittered on the frozen sea. A crack went zigzagging across the ice in front of them, and they jumped it, the sled bumping behind them. Then another crack, wider this time. The pugs veered away as the crack widened, but now more black cracks were widening all around them.

The ice of Kraken Deep jumped like a drumhead as the huge beast beneath it lurched upward, and all the tentacles writhed and strained.

The cracks yawned wider. The pugs stopped running. There was nowhere to run to; the sled was on an icy island, surrounded by widening cracks. The island began to tilt, and the sled slithered backward. Quickly, Shen leaned over the front of the sled and began unclipping the pugs' leashes. If the sled slid right over the edge of the ice and down into the dark water, he did not want it to drag all the poor pugs with it.

With a terrible splintering noise, one of the Kraken's tentacles tore free of the ice and came groping toward the stranded sled, showering Shen and Sika with cold salt water and shards of ice that smashed all around them like dropped windowpanes. The Kraken's huge eye watched coldly from below. It had been asleep for a long time—ever since the last True Winter, in fact. The runners of all the other sleds had woken it as they went skreeling across the ice. Now it was looking for its breakfast.

But the pugs were not having any of that.

They began to yip and yap even louder than before. They bounced about on their short legs, barking and snarling at the huge purple tentacle as it curled above them. One, braver than the rest, bounced so high that he managed to sink his teeth into the tip of it. The startled Kraken lashed its tentacle, but the pug clung on tight.

All the other pugs thought that looked like so much fun that they went charging off to find tentacles of their own to attack. Without the heavy sled to pull, they jumped easily over the cracks the Kraken had opened. Yipping fiercely, they flung themselves at the twining tentacles and bit them, hard.

The Kraken thrashed, trying to shake them off, but they just wagged their tails and snarled. The huge creature stared up through the ice in confusion. It had fought battles with killer whales in the dark blue depths and dragged polar bears down into its chilly lair, but it had never met creatures like these before. Little dark specks, like flakes of wind-blown fluff . . . but fluff with teeth!

Ow! thought the Kraken. And one by one, it snaked its tentacles back down into the deep. The pugs let go as the tentacle tips vanished back beneath the ice, but they kept barking and snarling and yipping.

Shen and Sika stared down through the ice. The great eye of the Kraken stared back angrily for a moment. Then it vanished as the Kraken squirted out a huge black cloud of ink to hide itself.

When the ink cleared, the Kraken was gone.

It had swum away to find a less dangerous breakfast—maybe a shark or two, out in the deep ocean. In the holes and cracks that it had made, the water was already freezing again.

"Phew!" said Shen. He started gathering the pugs together.

"Wait until I tell Grandpa!" said Sika. "That was as good as any of his stories!"

For the first time, Shen felt that there was a chance they might win. Then, while they were busy reattaching the pugs to the sled, they heard the barking of another dog team behind them. Shackleton Jones and SNOBOT had gotten their sled working again, and they came swooping across Kraken Deep, waving as they zipped past Shen and Sika.

"See?" shouted Shackleton Jones. "There's no Kraken here! It's all just a silly superstition!"

"But . . . ," Shen started to say.

It was no use. Already Shackleton Jones and his sled were just a dot, dwindling into the north.

"Great," said Sika. "Now we're last again!"

"But we have the bravest dog team," said Shen, scattering doggy treats for the pugs.

EIGHT

All through the night and all through the following day, the race ran on, and all sorts of adventures—and accidents—befell the other sleds.

Before long there were only five sleds left. Sir Basil Sprout-Dumpling was in the lead, thanks to a map his father had drawn that showed shortcuts between the rocks and islands of the frozen sea. But Helga Hammerfest was not far behind, and Mitzi von Primm and Shackleton Jones were catching up fast. (Shen and Sika were right at the back, of course, so far behind that the others didn't even know they were still in the race.)

On the third night, when Sideplate stopped the sled, Sir Basil could hear the baying of Mitzi's team behind him. It sounded as though she had overtaken Helga Hammerfest.

"Those pests are going to catch up to us, Sideplate!" he complained.

"Our lead does appear to be narrowing, sir," agreed Sideplate.

Sir Basil rubbed his mittens together gleefully. "Well, we'll soon get rid of them! Time for Operation Detour!"

"Are you sure that's necessary, sir?" asked Sideplate.

"Of course it is! If I don't make it to the Snowfather first, my fortune is finished! Get to work!"

Sideplate sighed and did as he was told. Out of the bundles at the front of Sir Basil's sled he fetched an inflatable signpost, which he pumped up with a bicycle pump.

"There!" said Sir Basil. "That should get rid of the others. You know where that will take them, Sideplate?"

"No, sir."

"Of course you don't! That's because I've been studying my dad's map and you haven't. It will lead them straight to the *Lost Hope*. Daddy saw it from a distance when he came this way all those years ago. He told me all about it. A few of the other competitors went to have a closer look, and they were never seen again!"

"How troubling, sir."

"Not for us it's not! The more racers we can get rid of, the easier we'll win. Come on, Sideplate—onward to the Pole!"

"Very good, sir," said Sideplate unhappily. He turned on the small portable snow machine on the back of Sir Basil's sled. White flakes covered its tracks as it sped away.

The sign stood where they had left it. Soon Mitzi von Primm's sled came speeding up, turned sharp left, and followed Sir Basil's detour. Close behind came Helga Hammerfest, who also turned left. Then a little later, Shackleton Jones arrived.

"Thin ice, eh?" he said. "Better take the detour, SNOBOT."

"I am not detecting thin ice ahead," said the robot. "It is safe to proceed due north."

"Hmm. Still, better not take any chances, eh?"

After that, it was very quiet for a long

GREAT PERIL!

THIN ICE AHEAD!

PROBABLY OTHER SCARY THINGS TOO

DANGER

time. The night grew colder and colder. It grew so cold that pieces of the northern lights froze and fell out of the sky. They lay strewn about on the ice, glowing gently.

At last Shen and Sika arrived at the detour sign.

If Sika had been driving, she would have known at once that the detour was a trick. Her grandpa had told her enough

DETOUR

stories of his race that she knew there was no such thing as thin ice, not that far north, not in a True Winter.

But Sika was not driving. Sika was asleep, wrapped up in furs, leaning against one of the sled's carved totems. And when Shen saw the sign, he turned left at once, following the tracks of all the other sleds.

The paws of the scampering pugs kicked up a mist of powdered ice. It blew into Sika's sleeping face and woke her. She saw the big gold moon lying on the horizon far ahead and knew at once that they were going the wrong way.

"Why have we turned?"

Shen explained.

"That can't be right!" she said. "We must turn back!"

Shen tried to turn the sled. But by then the pugs were moving more and more slowly. That last burst of speed that woke Sika had tired them out. The sled came slowly to a halt, and the little dogs flopped down in sleepy heaps.

"We can't go any farther tonight," said Shen.

He got down from the sled and started to get food for the dogs. While they ate, he and Sika put up Grandpa's old tent. They hammered the iron tent pegs deep into the ice in case a storm blew up while they were sleeping. When they had all had something to eat, Shen and Sika crawled inside the tent and called the dogs in after them. They snuggled down in their sleeping bags, the sleepy pugs

piled over them, and in a short time Shen was sleeping, too.

But Sika could not sleep. She looked at the embroidered patterns on the walls of the tent. A fallen northern light had wedged in a snowdrift nearby, and it glowed gently through the canvas. And from somewhere not so nearby, very faintly through the frozen air, came singing.

Sika slid out from under her blanket of pugs. (They were so fast asleep that they did not notice her leaving.) She went outside into the glowing night and started walking toward the sound of the singing. If she had looked behind her as she walked, she would have seen that her footprints were quietly closing up, leaving snow that was smooth and white as empty pages. (There are fifty different types of snow in a True Winter, and this was blindsnow— the type that hides all tracks.)

But Sika was not looking behind her. She kept her eyes on a jagged hill of shattered rock ahead. (It would have been an island if the sea had been water instead of ice.) It seemed to her that the singing was coming from behind it. A green glow shone from behind it, too, as if a really big bit of the northern lights had fallen there.

She scrambled up between the rocks and looked. There stood a huge old ship, completely trapped in the ice. The name painted on its rusty stern said *Hope*, and suddenly Sika remembered something her grandpa had told her, about how a lot of the teams he had raced against had gotten sidetracked somewhere called "The Lost Hope" and were never seen again. She hadn't realized that the *Lost Hope* was a ship.

She went a little closer.

Parked beside the ship were three sleds.

There was the high-tech sled of Shackleton Jones, with its robot dogs waiting motionless. Next to it stood the ancient bog-oak sled of Helga Hammerfest, and Mitzi von Primm's pink designer sled. Mitzi's dog team and Helga's polar bears snoozed beside them, but there was no sign of their owners.

Above the sleds, fragments of fallen northern lights had been hung up along the *Lost Hope*'s rusty side. That was where the green glow came from. The lights spelled out three words.

"What a strange place for a noodle bar," she said to herself. "Who would sell noodles all the way out here?"

A huge, hairy white hand reached out from behind a rock and grabbed her by the hood of her coat. A huge, hairy white voice rumbled in her ear.

"YETIS WOULD."

NINE

No one knew how the yetis had come to that place. Had they arrived with the good ship *Hope* when it ran aground and was abandoned there? Or had they come loping across the frozen sea one True Winter and decided that the wreck of the *Lost Hope* would be a good place to live?

As for what had given them the idea to open a noodle bar—well, that was easy. There are fifty different types of snow in a True Winter, and the type that fell on that island was a very special type that could be made into beautiful noodles. (It made very nice spaghetti, too, but the yetis had decided that Yeti Spaghetti Bar sounded too obvious.)

At first Sika was a little bit scared at being captured by a yeti, but when she realized that it only wanted her to come and eat some noodles, she calmed down. She really liked noodles. The yeti took her by the hand and led her across the snow toward the ship. It was a large yeti and looked very yeti-ish, with long white hair, big feet, glowing eyes—you know the type.

As Sika followed the yeti up the side of the ship, she wondered if she should tell it that Shen was nearby and ask it if she could go and get him so that he could have some noodles, too. Then she decided to wait until she had tried them herself. They might be gross, and nobody likes to be woken up in the middle of the night for gross noodles.

The decks of the *Lost Hope* were glassy

with ice, but down inside, in the old ballroom, there was warmth and light. Candles made from yeti earwax flickered there, and a yeti-dung fire burned merrily in an igloo-shaped stove. Long tables had been set up in the middle of the ballroom. There sat Mitzi von Primm, Helga Hammerfest, Shackleton Jones, and a whole load of yetis, all digging into big bowls of snow noodles, while yetis wearing flowery aprons carried yet more noodles in through the swinging doors that led to the kitchen. These doors had round glass windows in them.

Sika peeked through as her yeti dragged her past them. She saw yetis shoveling snow out of big buckets while others packed it into fat snowballs and stuffed them into a mincing machine. They all took turns to crank the handle of the machine, and the long white noodles came writhing out of it like worms. And as the yetis worked, they sang:

WE'RE IN THE MOODLES
THE MOODLES FOR SOME NOODLES
NO RUSKS OR APPLE STRUDELS
WHICH ARE ONLY FIT FOR POODLES
WE DON'T MEAN TO BE RUDLES
WE JUST WANT OUR FAVORITE FOODLES
NOODLES!
NOODLES!
NOODLES!

Sika's yeti pulled out a chair for her and sat her down between Mitzi von Primm and Shackleton Jones. From the other table, Helga Hammerfest called, "Yoo-hoo! Welcome to the *Lost Hope*, Sika! You must try these noodles!"

"They're delicious!" agreed Mitzi von Primm. "But I mustn't have any more. I'm watching my figure."

"Delicious indeed!" agreed Shackleton Jones. "But I'd best be on my way. I still mean to beat you good people to the top of the world!"

But just then, a yeti plonked a big dish of noodles down on the table, and Mitzi and Shackleton took huge helpings for themselves, just like everybody else. Sika took some, too. She was surprised how nice they tasted. She had expected them to be a little ... well ... snowy, but they weren't; they were hot and nutty and delicious.

For a while the only sounds in the old ship were of people and yetis chewing and swallowing and saying "Mmmm." Oh, and one other sound: a small voice, urgently buzzing, like a very polite alarm clock.

"Something's wrong," said SNOBOT, looking up at Sika from under the table. "These noodles are a little too tempting. That dummy Shackleton's been here for hours now, eating and eating them. It's as if he's forgotten all about reaching the top of the world. And he doesn't even like noodles!"

Sika thought about that. It did sound as if something strange was going on, but it was hard to work out what, because the noodles tasted so lovely that they kept distracting her.

"These must be MIND-CONTROLLING NOODLES!" SNOBOT was saying. "The yetis mean to keep you all here as their slaves!"

"Mmmm," said Sika, helping herself to

some more noodles. And then suddenly all the noodles were gone!

"More noodles!" roared the yetis at the table, and their human guests all joined in. "More noodles!"

"Just coming," said one of the yeti chefs, gathering up their empty bowls and the dirty forks, spoons, and chopsticks. "But first, you travelers must pay for the noodles you've already eaten."

"What?" cried Mitzi. "You never said anything about paying. . . ."

"You didn't think they'd be free, did you?" growled the yetis. "The sign outside says Noodle Bar, not Free Noodles."

"Do you take major credit cards?" asked Shackleton Jones.

"Cash only," said the yeti chef, and the other yetis rose to their feet and looked down menacingly at their guests, who suddenly felt very small and a little frightened and yet, at the same time, still hungry for more noodles.

"If they can't pay," said one of the yetis, "there's only one thing for it. They're going to have to . . . *do the dishes!*"

He kicked open the double doors into the

kitchen. The last time she peeked in, Sika had been too interested by the snow-into-noodles machine to notice much else. Now she saw that the far side of the kitchen, where the sink was, was piled from floor to ceiling with teetering stacks of bowls, plates, jugs, saucepans, forks, spoons, and trays, all smeared and crusted with years of dried-on pieces of noodle.

Those yetis loved making noodles, and they loved eating noodles, but they absolutely HATED washing up.

"Do the dishes!" they chanted, picking up their human captives and carrying them toward the kitchen. "Do the dishes!"

And the humans were too full of noodles, and too afraid that the yetis might not allow them any *more* noodles, to resist.

So this is why no one ever returned from the Lost Hope, thought Sika as big yeti hands lifted her out of her chair and carried her

119

toward the kitchen. *They get lured in with noodles, and then have to stay here, washing up for the rest of their lives!*

She looked around and saw SNOBOT watching her. He wasn't at all interested in noodles, so the yetis weren't interested in him. She beckoned him closer, and while her yeti was lining up to carry her into the kitchen after the others, she whispered quickly, "Shen's camped not far away! Tell him not to come here! Tell him to keep going! All the way to the top of the world!"

SNOBOT hurried off on his mechanical legs. The yeti lurched into the kitchen with Sika, and the doors swung shut behind her.

TEN

Shen was back on the *Lucky Star,* sailing homeward on a warm and sunny evening, and all the pugs were crowding at the ship's prow, wagging their tails and watching for the first sight of land. But just as he was about to dig into the nice fat ice cream that Captain Jeggings had handed him, an icy breeze began to blow. The top blew off the ice cream and landed in Shen's face, which woke him up.

"Yuck! Brrr!" he said.

The tent flap was open, and SNOBOT was leaning over him. The robot was covered

in snow, and a big dollop had just dropped off him and landed in Shen's face. Shen sat up, wiping it away.

"What are you doing here?" he asked. "Where's Sika?"

SNOBOT explained.

Kidnapped by yetis??? Shen wondered if he should just harness up the pugs and sled off fast, before the yetis caught him, too.

But no. Sika was his friend. She was the first real friend he had ever had. "Friends don't leave friends behind to wash dishes for yetis!" he said. "We have to do something!"

But what?

He wiggled out from under the sleepy pugs and went outside. How clear and cold it was! He could hear the gruff singing of the yetis coming from behind the rocky island. He woke the pugs and harnessed them to the sled, but he did not get aboard it; he just wanted it to be ready if he needed to make a quick getaway. Then he set off on foot, tramping around the end of the island. The pugs followed him, with SNOBOT perching on the sled as it shushed along behind them, leaving no tracks in the blindsnow.

Then they hit a patch of a different type of snow. It sang in a little squeaky voice each time Shen put his foot down, and when SNOBOT and the pugs and the sled hit it, it sounded like a snowy opera.

"Shhhh!" hissed Shen, afraid that the singing snow would warn the yetis somebody was coming.

"Shhhh!" said a patch of snow nearby.

"Who said that?" whispered Shen.

"Who said that?" said the snow quite loudly. It was echosnow, which repeats anything you say to it, only louder. It started all the pugs yipping, and the echosnow yipped back at them more loudly, which made the pugs yip louder still. Shen stood in a storm

of yips and waited for the yetis to come and find him.

But the yetis were far too busy enjoying themselves. It was a big treat for them when newcomers arrived and they had someone else to do the washing up for a change. They had locked the doors of the kitchen, and they were all outside on the deck, bathing in the green glow of the northern lights and singing their yeti songs.

After a while, when he realized that the yetis were not going to come for him, Shen had an idea. He tiptoed over to the patch of echosnow and started clumping it into snowballs. He showed SNOBOT how to make snowballs, too, and together they quickly piled the sled high with them. Then they hurried on toward the *Lost Hope*. While SNOBOT took the sled to where the other sleds were parked and started getting them ready to leave, Shen went around to the other side of the old ship alone. From there he could see the big, shaggy shapes of the yetis above him, dancing on the icy deck. He could also see a steamed-up porthole that must have been the kitchen, where the washing up was happening.

Shen picked up a snowball and threw it as hard as he could at the yetis. It was a brilliant shot, and it hit the biggest yeti right in the face. The yeti roared:

"WHO THREW THAT?"

"It was me!" whispered Shen, throwing another snowball.

"It was me!" shouted the snowball, landing behind the yetis. They turned to see who had spoken. Shen whispered, "Over here!" and threw another.

it called, hitting the biggest yeti's head.

The biggest yeti scowled at the others.

"It wasn't us!" they said.

said a snowball, landing out of sight.

 YOU BIG HAIRBALL!

said another snowball.

The biggest yeti pulled some snow out of his fur and squeezed it into a snowball. The others scooped snow off the decks and the roofs of the cabins. Soon the air on deck was full of flying snowballs as the yetis pelted each other.

Shen kept throwing snowballs, too. "Missed me!" Shen's snowballs jeered, and "Hey, Fur Face! Over here!"

And the yetis picked up the burst balls of echosnow and made fresh snowballs from them, and the echosnow echoed their own angry shouts as well as the things that Shen was whispering. Before long the snowball fight had turned into a full-scale snowball battle.

None of the yetis noticed a small boy scrambling up the side of their old ship and knocking on the kitchen porthole.

The poor washer-uppers inside had not thought to open that porthole. Helga Hammerfest and Mitzi von Primm and Shackleton Jones could never have squeezed out through it, and Sika was too busy drying to have even noticed it. Shen tumbled in, bringing a cold blast of air with him, which startled the washer-uppers to their senses.

"The yetis are having a snowball fight! SNOBOT is waiting with the sleds. We must leave quickly!" He stopped, his mouth hanging open, staring at the grown-ups. Was it just his imagination, or had they changed?

Sika saw it, too, now. Helga Hammerfest had always had a beard, but it had not been quite that long before, or quite that soft, and it had not been white. Shackleton Jones had a white beard, too, and white side whiskers, and bushy white eyebrows. But it was Mitzi von Primm who had changed most of all. She had put on so much weight that her pink designer racing outfit was starting to split at the seams. Her face and hands were covered with soft white fur, and her eyes glowed blue.

"They're turning into yetis!" said Shen.

"It must be a side effect of the noodle-snow!" said Sika, and she checked her reflection in the bottom of a freshly cleaned saucepan to see if she was turning into a yeti, too. She wasn't, which was a relief. She supposed it must have been because the others had all been eating at the *Lost Hope* for much longer than her, and they had eaten way more noodles.

"That must be who these yetis are!" she said. "They are the sailors from the *Lost Hope*, and other poor souls who have happened by, all transformed by eating noodlesnow. . . ."

"Mmmm, lovely, lovely noodles," said Mitzi von Primm, stroking her own soft white fur.

Shackleton Jones said, "That is completely impossible! How could anyone turn into a yeti? Most unscientific, I say." Then he caught sight of his own reflection in the pan that Sika held up in front of him. "Aaaargh!" he shrieked. "I don't want to be a yeti!"

His shriek startled Helga Hammerfest from her own trance. "Neither do I," she said. "There was something . . . something I had to do . . . that's right . . . the race! I was on my way to the North Pole. . . ."

"Then you'd better get out of here and stop eating noodlesnow!" said Shen.

"But the doors are locked!" complained Sika.

"Helga," said Shen, "you can open them, can't you?"

Helga stomped over to the doors and leaned on them with all her weight. There was quite a lot of Helga's weight, and the doors smashed open easily. They all ran out into the ballroom, past the empty tables. All except Mitzi, who stopped to pick up a few stray noodles that had fallen on one of the tables.

"Come on!" shouted Sika.

"And don't eat any more of those!" cried Shackleton Jones.

"But I like them!" said Mitzi, slurping the noodles up. "And I like being a yeti. Look at my lovely silky fur!" And she shook off the tatters of her racing outfit and stretched out her long white hairy arms, admiring the way the candlelight shone on her pelt.

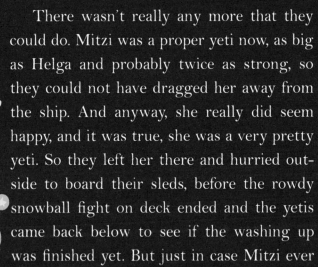

"She had more noodles than any of us," said Helga.

"But, Mitzi, what about the race?" asked Shen. "What about the Snowfather's palace? Don't you want to be the first to reach the top of the world?"

"Oh, you go on without me," said Mitzi happily. "I'm going to simply love being a yeti, and I already have my wish—all the lovely noodles I can eat."

There wasn't really any more that they could do. Mitzi was a proper yeti now, as big as Helga and probably twice as strong, so they could not have dragged her away from the ship. And anyway, she really did seem happy, and it was true, she was a very pretty yeti. So they left her there and hurried outside to board their sleds, before the rowdy snowball fight on deck ended and the yetis came back below to see if the washing up was finished yet. But just in case Mitzi ever decided she had had enough of yeti-ing, they left her sled behind, and Shackleton Jones left her his robot huskies and harnessed her team to his high-tech sled.

"This is SO embarrassing," SNOBOT said, cracking his whip above the heads of the pink pooches.

"Not as embarrassing as losing the race will be!" called Helga as her polar bear–powered sled went racing past him. Now that the spell of the noodles had faded, she was re-membering how much she wanted to win the race. She waved to Shen and Sika. "Thanks, kiddies! I'll see you at the top of the world!"

"Jeepers, SNOBOT!" shouted Shackleton Jones. "Let's get moving, or the bearded lady will be there before us!"

And pretty soon both their sleds were just dots in the distance, and Shen and Sika were losing the race again.

ELEVEN

The days that followed weren't really days at all; sunrise was just a faint silvering of light upon the southern sky. The pugs ran north as fast as their two hundred sixty-four little legs could carry them, following the tracks of the other sleds.

There are fifty different types of snow in a True Winter, and Shen and Sika had soon seen nearly all of them.

They crossed patches of blindsnow and patches of echosnow. They plunged through

warbling drifts of songsnow and scream-
ing mounds of screechsnow. They crossed a
broad, rolling plain of slumbersnow, which
snored and mumbled and farted like someone
asleep under a huge white comforter.

Helga and the rest were so far ahead now
that it barely seemed worth going on. How
could Sika and Shen hope to reach the North
Pole first? But Sika said they had to try.
"Maybe the other sleds will all drop out,"
she said. "Or hit a patch of shrinksnow and

be miniaturized, or a patch of stonesnow and be turned to statues. . . ."

After that, Shen kept a look out for statues and miniature sleds, but he didn't see any, just the tracks of the other racers, leading endlessly on over the horizon.

They came to a waste of weresnow, which kept shaping itself into snowmen when they weren't looking. They would stop the sled for a while to look at the compass or cook food on their camping stove and look up to find that they were surrounded by a ring of snowmen. And these weren't nice snowmen with scarves and carrots for noses. Oh no. These were horrible snowmen with sharp, icy teeth and frozen claws and open, hungry mouths.

141

It was all very unsettling.

Before long, Shen and Sika were so tired of being unsettled that they almost thought of turning back. But the pugs weren't frightened of the weresnow, not even when it tried forming itself into scary snowdogs. The pugs just yipped at them, and eventually some of the braver ones started biting the snowmen's snowy bottoms. After that the weresnow stopped its tricks, though Shen and Sika could still feel it sulking at them as they sped on into the north.

But there was not a lot of north left to speed on into now. Pretty soon they would reach the top of the world, from where, whichever way you go, you're going south. As the last silver smear of the short day faded behind them, they saw something glinting and glittering far ahead. It was the northern lights reflecting on the frosty spires of the Snowfather's palace.

Grrrrrr

"We've done it!" said Sika. "We're nearly there!"

"But I bet one of the others has gotten there already," Shen said. He thought that if he kept saying that, it would not be so disappointing if they found that Helga, Shackleton Jones, or Sir Basil was already there. But he could not help hoping, secretly, that Sika was right. They could still be first, if only something had delayed the other racers.

And after a little while longer, when they had crossed a particularly smelly patch of stinksnow, they found that something *had*.

The Snowfather's palace was not far off now. They could see it sitting there on the horizon like a gigantic, beautiful igloo. But between them and the palace was a deep chasm. The chasm's walls seemed to reach all the way down to the floor of the sea. Across the chasm, like a web of lace, there stretched a maze of snow bridges.

"It's beautiful!" said Shen.

"But I'm not sure it can take our weight . . . ," said Sika.

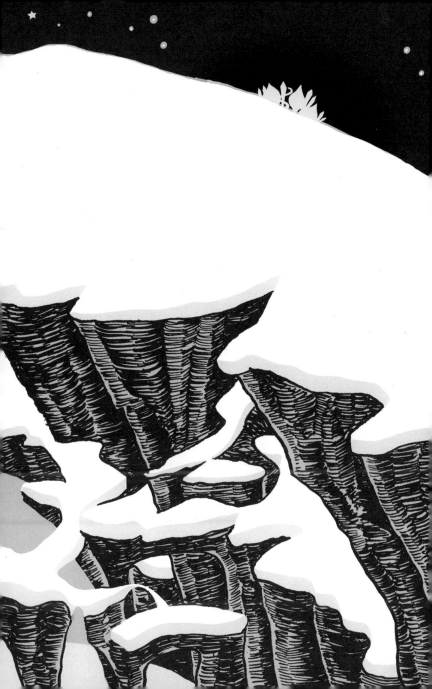

Very slowly, very carefully, they steered the sled onto one of the bridges. It trembled and creaked, and chunks of snow dropped from its underside and tumbled down into the shadows at the bottom of the abyss. Shen peered down after them and saw spiky white shapes moving down there. Snowtrolls, waiting to eat anyone who fell . . .

"Help!" cried a voice, echoing between the leaping arches and tall, spindly pillars of the snow. The northern lights were pulsing

brightly overhead, and by their glow the children saw Helga Hammerfest.

Poor Helga! She had done her best to stick to the thickest bridges, but even so her mighty bog-oak sled had been too heavy. The middle of one of the bridges had dropped out as she tried to cross it. Her polar bears, Snowdrop and Slushpuppy, sat unhappily on the far side of the gap. The sled, which was still attached to them, dangled in midair above the chasm. Helga dangled from the sternpost of the sled.

She had tied herself on to it with her beard.

From time to time, Snowdrop and Slushpuppy scrambled to their feet and tried to heave the sled up. It would rise a few feet, but it was too heavy for them to drag it back onto the bridge. Each time they tried, more snow fell from the bridge, spattering Helga and her sled and then tumbling down into the depths.

Shen and Sika looked at each other. It would have been easy to keep going, but they could not leave Helga hanging there.

"Mush!" shouted Shen, and the pugs surged. Shen and Sika's sled was so much lighter than Helga's, and the pugs were so much lighter than polar bears, that even the flimsiest of the bridges could hold them. They threaded their way across the maze until they were on the part of the broken bridge where Snowdrop and Slushpuppy sat.

"Thank you, children!" Helga shouted, from down in the blue depths of the chasm.

"Please cut my poor polar bears loose. They're getting tired, and I don't want them to fall along with me."

"No!" called Shen. "We're going to pull you up!"

"Boo!" shouted the snowtrolls, down in the shadows below. They had been looking forward to Helga falling so that they could eat her. They started hurling big splinters of ice up at the bridge, hoping to dislodge her before Shen and Sika could save her. But the abyss was deep, and the trolls were horrible throwers, so the shards all fell back harmlessly.

Shen started unhitching the pugs from Sika's sled and tying their leashes to Snowdrop's and Slushpuppy's harnesses. The polar bears sniffed curiously at their new teammates. If they had been hungry, they could have eaten the sixty-six little dogs in sixty-six big bites and then had Shen and Sika for dessert. But they were unusually well-trained polar bears, and they seemed to understand that Shen and Sika and those small yipping creatures were there to help.

It took a while, but eventually all the pugs were attached. "Mush!" shouted Sika. The pugs strained forward, pulling the polar bears. The polar bears strained forward, pulling the dangling sled. Inch by inch it rose, until it was jammed against the crumbling end of the

broken snow bridge. Then Helga untied
her beard and scrambled up the sled as if
it were a ladder. Gasping and panting, she heaved herself up onto
the bridge.

The exhausted pugs
relaxed, and then the
sled dropped again,
dragging the polar
bears and pugs
back with it. Just
in time, Helga
pulled a big knife
from under her
furs and slashed

through Snowdrop's and Slushpuppy's harnesses. The sled dropped silently for a long time, and then, from far below, they heard the deep, echoey crash as it smashed to pieces in the bottom of the chasm. "Boo!" and "Spoilsports!" bellowed the trolls, annoyed that nobody had been on it when it fell.

It seemed wrong to leave Helga behind, even though she had left them behind back at the *Lost Hope*. So they made her sit with Shen on the sled, and Sika went ahead and tested the snow bridges with a stick while Snowdrop and Slushpuppy walked behind. And they had not gone far when they heard another voice calling, "Help!"

Shackleton Jones had had the opposite trouble. He had chosen to cross the maze by the fastest route, across the thinnest and most fragile bridges. He was sure that his super-lightweight sled would not collapse them. But he had forgotten that the pink huskies that were pulling it weighed more than the robot dogs he had left behind. The frailest of the bridges had crumbled beneath the pink dogs' paws, and now they hung from their harnesses, with only the weight of the sled, Shackleton, and SNOBOT to stop them from falling into the chasm. Below them, more hungry trolls were piling up a tower of snow to try to reach the dangling dogs.

"Can you help us, please?" the scientist shouted when he saw Shen and Sika's sled passing. "I can't cut these poor doggies loose!"

The trolls' tower was almost tall enough by the time the racers reached him. A troll climbed to the top of it and, standing on tiptoe, managed to grab the pink pom-pom on one of the dogs' tails. Then it was snatched out of his hand as Shen, Sika, and Helga all helped Shackleton and SNOBOT heave the dogs back onto the bridge.

"Spoilsports!" shouted the trolls.

Shen and Sika went on their way, with Shackleton Jones following. Once or twice he eyed the maze ahead as if he were thinking of ways to get past the children and beat them to the Snowfather's palace, but Helga said, "Don't even think about it! That's twice those kids have saved us."

Soon they were nearing the far side of the chasm. And there ahead of them, going carefully across one final bridge, was the sled of Sir Basil Sprout-Dumpling.

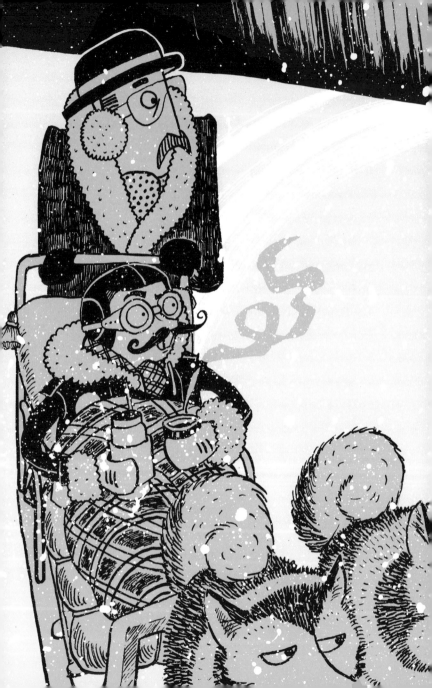

TWELVE

S ir Basil looked back and saw the procession that was following him—Sika with her testing stick, the pugs, the pink huskies, the two sleds and two polar bears, Shen, Helga, Shackleton Jones, and SNOBOT.

"Look, Sideplate! They've almost caught up to us!"

"Indeed, Sir Basil. The crossing of the snow bridges has lost us a great deal of time, sir."

Sir Basil looked ahead. He saw the wide plain of ice that still separated him from the palace of the Snowfather. Plenty of room on a plain like that for those kids to slip ahead

159

of him! Those pugs of theirs were better sled dogs than he'd thought, and he knew that Shackleton's high-tech sled was speedier than his.

"I think it's time for some more dirty tricks, Sideplate!"

"Oh, dear, sir," said Sideplate. "Are you sure that's necessary, sir?"

"Well, of course it is!"

Sir Basil laughed a wicked laugh and twirled his mustache, but it had frozen solid and he snapped the end off. Sideplate, sighing sadly, opened Sir Basil's expensive antique gun case and lifted out Sir Basil's expensive antique rocket launcher.

"I really must protest, Sir Basil," he said as he handed it over. "Your behavior is most unsporting. When we return to London, I shall give you my resignation, sir."

"Do whatever you like, Sideplate," sneered Sir Basil, getting the rocket launcher ready and pointing it at the snow bridge that the others were just about to cross. "I will have had my wish granted by then. I'll be the richest man in the world, and I'll be able to hire billions of better butlers than you, you fool."

"Very good, sir," said Sideplate. He winced as Sir Basil pulled the trigger and a rocket went shooting toward the snow bridge.

Shen winced, too, ducking as the rocket swerved over his head in a rush of sparks and smoke. Sir Basil had terrible aim. He had missed the bridge completely! But the rocket hit one of the other bridges, way off at the far side of the chasm. The bridge burst apart and fell into the depths, and the bridge next to it began to crumble, too, and then two more bridges joined in. The whole beautiful maze of bridges began to quiver, and sag, and crumble, and collapse.

161

"Quick!" shouted Sika, running down the last bridge.

"Quick—I mean, MUSH!" shouted Shen, urging the pugs after her.

The others followed, as quickly as they dared—Shackleton Jones and his pink team, SNOBOT, and Helga and her two bears. Behind them, the final bridge was disintegrating with a rush and a roar of falling snow.

For a moment Shen was sure that they were all going to fall into the chasm and be eaten by the snow-trolls, whom he could hear jeering and cheering down there. Then he saw that the end of the bridge was only a few yards away and that they were going to make it after all. And then he noticed that Sir Basil was taking aim with another rocket, and this time the travelers were so close that Shen was pretty sure he couldn't miss.

"Take this, you scum!" sneered Sir Basil.

But just as he pulled the trigger, Sideplate's snow boot kicked the rocket launcher upward. The rocket whizzed harmlessly off into the sky, to burst somewhere among the northern lights.

"Sideplate, you spoilsport!" spluttered Sir Basil.

The bridges were still crumbling, filling the air above the chasm with a haze of powdered snow. Sideplate ran to meet Sika and the others as they came spilling onto the ice. The bridge they'd just crossed disintegrated behind them, almost taking Shackleton Jones with it, but he and SNOBOT managed to leap to safety as their sled dropped into the chasm. Helga quickly cut the pink dogs' harnesses to stop them from going with it.

"I must apologize for Sir Basil's behavior, ladies and gentlemen," said Sideplate, helping Shackleton Jones climb over the edge of the chasm. "He has always been most unsporting."

"So long, Sideplate!" called Sir Basil, leaping aboard his sled. "I'll go even faster without you!" His long whip cracked above his huskies' ears, and they started to run toward the far-off igloo palace. But just then, with a massive thump, a big, jagged, glowing thing came slamming down, smashing the sled to

pieces and catapulting Sir Basil high into the air. That last rocket had done a lot of damage when it exploded up there among the northern lights; now broken shards of light were dropping all around, freezing as they plummeted through the chilly sky.

Shen and his friends waited until the rain of broken lights was over, then picked their way between the shards to where Sir Basil's sled lay splintered. Sideplate disentangled the dogs, who ran off in all directions woofing happily.

Sir Basil had landed in a deep drift of snow. He scrambled out, shouting more threats and shaking his fist. But his fist seemed smaller than before. All of him did. He was dwindling before their eyes, shrinking down and down until he was no bigger than a toy soldier, while his voice grew higher and higher. "You menacing morons! Look what you've made me do! I've fallen into a patch of shrinksnow!"

"Careful!" said Helga, lassoing the tiny cheat with a pug leash. "We mustn't touch that patch of snow ourselves."

"If those little dogs got any smaller, we might not be able to see them at all!" said Shackleton Jones.

Helga reeled Sir Basil in, until he was close enough for her to reach out and pick him up. He kept being terribly rude at first, until he realized just how tiny he'd become. Then he said, "Oh . . . ah . . . no hard feelings, right?"

"Is there a cure for shrinksnow?" asked Shen.

"I don't know," said Shackleton Jones. "The effects may wear off eventually."

"But I can't stay this size forever!" wailed Sir Basil. Helga handed him to Sideplate, who put him in a lunch box for safekeeping (making sure to punch some airholes in the lid first). They could hear his tiny, angry voice buzzing in there as they set off again toward the icicle palace.

It wasn't really a race anymore; they all just felt that, having come so far, they should at least say hello to the Snowfather. There was not enough room on the sled for all of them, so they took turns walking. It was hard work, crossing that ice, for it was very slippery, and although it had looked flat from the snow bridges, it actually sloped very steeply upward.

And as they trudged up that slope, so it grew colder. Shen didn't think it could get any colder, but it did. He had grown used to seeing his breath come out as steam, but at the top of the world each steamy breath froze solid as soon as he breathed it and fell on the ice in front of him with a little tinkly sound like a dropped ornament. It was so cold that the pugs, who had run so far and so bravely in their little sweaters, began to shiver, and their tiny feet grew numb, and soon they could barely walk at all. Then Sideplate and Helga gathered them up, and Helga wrapped them all in her beard, which was still extravagantly long and white and warm after her meal of yeti noodles back at the *Lost Hope*. Their little faces peeked out as she plodded onward, and

Sika, Shen, and Shackleton harnessed the two polar bears and the pink huskies and Sir Basil's dogs to the sled instead.

"Soon it will be too cold to talk," Shen started to say. But already it was too cold to talk; he decided to keep his mouth shut, in case his tongue froze solid like a pink Popsicle.

And then it was too cold to think. It was as if the ice had gotten inside his head, and all his thoughts slowed down and stopped, like fish frozen in the sea.

But he kept trudging on, putting one cold foot in front of the other, and suddenly he felt the cold ease a little, and then a little more. And he raised his eyes—which had been watching only the ice in front of him—and there was the igloo palace of the

171

Snowfather towering up into the sky in front of him, a huge dome of snow, with spires and towers and turrets sprouting all around it, and snow chimneys sending up little curls of smoke to tangle in the northern lights. And sitting in front of the high white wall that ran around the icicle palace was a huge old man, bigger even than Sika's grandpa.

"I'm so glad you made it!" he said, and his voice was warm and rich like a wintertime dessert. "Now, which of you is the winner? Whose wish shall I grant?"

THIRTEEN

For a moment, nobody spoke except for Sir Basil, who said, "Me! I'm the winner, of course!" But he was so muffled inside the box that the Snowfather didn't hear him.

In the end, it was Shen who said, "None of us is the winner."

"That's true," said Sika. "We all got here together, and none of us could have made it without the others. I'd still be washing up for the yetis if SNOBOT hadn't gone and roused Shen. . . ."

"We'd all *be* yetis if Shen hadn't rescued us," said Shackleton.

175

"And I'd have fallen into the chasm if Shen and Sika hadn't helped me," Helga said. "They were very brave."

"And the pugs would have frozen if Helga hadn't nestled them in her beard."

"And then we would all have been blown up by Sir Basil's rocket if Sideplate hadn't so kindly saved us."

"So none of us is the winner," said Shen sadly. "Not really."

The Snowfather's wide white grin grew wider still. "Or maybe ALL of you are the winners," he said. "For the first time ever, I declare the race a tie. So come inside, and let us discuss the matter of prizes. . . ."

They followed him through the gate in the high white wall into a garden. Green was the last color they had expected to see here at the top of the world, but green was all around them—the glowing greens of grass and trees, speckled with red and golden flowers.

"How did you grow all these plants?" asked Shackleton Jones.

"I didn't grow them," said the Snowfather. "I made them! Out of snow!"

"Snow?" said Sideplate, reaching out to run his hands over a tree trunk.

"Everything you see here is made of snow," said the Snowfather. "The special anything-snow that falls only here, at the top of the world. Shape it into whatever you want, and it will become real."

He strode over to a drift of snow that had gathered against the wall of his igloo. Kneeling, he scooped some up and made it into a little snow bird. "There!" he said. And as they watched, the white bird blushed and darkened, opened its black-bead eyes, and flittered away to perch singing on the branch of a tree. "Whatever you like!" he said.

For a moment everyone was too amazed to speak.

Then, with whoops and cheers, the travelers all threw themselves at that mound of snow and started to help themselves to clumps of it and shape those clumps into—well, whatever they could imagine. Shen made a little snow ship, which turned into the most perfect little real ship he had ever seen, complete with rigging and anchor chains and all sorts of things he hadn't been able to sculpt in snow, but that the snow knew he had wanted anyway. He put

it in his pocket and set to work making a

snow treasure chest and filling it with snowy diamonds.

"Ah, that's what Sir Basil's father did, when he came here all those years ago," said Sideplate. He was busy making a snow bowler hat to replace his own, which was looking a bit battered after all his adventures.

Meanwhile, Shackleton Jones was making snow cogs

and snow wheels, the snowy parts for some snow machine. And Helga was sculpting a  big heap of snow into the shape of a polar bear— which shook it-self, roared, and went running off across the lawn to play with Snow-drop and Slush-puppy and the sixty-six pugs. "You can never have too many friendly polar bears," said Helga.

And Sika? She just sat and watched, and the Snowfather sat beside her, chuckling at the delight of the others as they busied themselves making snow things. "Always the same," he said. "Ever since Ooka first came here and discovered the anythingsnow."

"What did she make?" asked Sika.

"Ah," said the Snowfather, "she was feeling rather lonely, having come so far all by herself, so she made a snowman. She didn't even know it was anythingsnow she was making him from, but she lay down to sleep beside him, and when she woke up . . ."

"He had come alive?" asked Sika.

The Snowfather smiled and nodded, remembering.

"And what about you, young Sika?" he asked. "What will you make?"

"I don't know," said Sika. "The thing I want isn't a thing. I came here to ask if you could make my grandpa better."

"Oh, my dear," said the Snowfather gently, "I'm afraid that is a bit beyond me."

"But you grant wishes, don't you? That's what all the stories say. They say you'll give the winner their heart's desire."

"I think there's been a bit of a mix-up, then," said the Snowfather. "I am the guardian of the anythingsnow, but I cannot grant wishes. If people have gotten their heart's desire by coming here, then either their heart's desire was something they could make out of snow, or it was something that they found along the way, like your grandpa did."

"Do you remember my grandpa?"

"Of course I do! Such a brave boy he was. I hoped he'd win, but Sir Basil's father beat him in the end. (I suspect Sir Basil's father was a cheat, like his son.) But it did not matter! Your grandpa didn't need to fill his pockets with snow jewels. Just the journeying here was prize enough for him; just to see all the wonders of True Winter and go home with stories to tell."

"Such stories!" said Sika. "And when he dies, there will be no more."

"No, no," said the Snowfather. "All old things die in the end, but not stories. Stories go on and on, and new ones are always being born. Now, join the others, before the snow is all used up."

So Sika ran to join the fun. Shen had finished his chest of snow diamonds and squeezed the lid shut, and he was busy making

sixty-six snow bones for the sixty-six pugs. Sika helped, and while she was at it she thought of a few things that she had always wanted, too, and together they made those out of snow.

And then everyone remembered how hungry they were, and they started making snow food that they carried inside and ate in a huge feast beside the Snowfather's roaring snow-log fire. And while they ate, they all talked about what they were going to do next.

"I've got my wish," said Shackleton Jones. "SNOBOT has collected enough data and samples of these strange types of snow that I'll be kept busy for years. I'll be famous! I'll

probably get a snowflake named after me. And I'm going to call in at the *Lost Hope* on my way home. It seems to me that what those yetis really need is an electric dishwasher, and I'm just the man to make it for them."

"I'm going to buy Sir Basil's stately home," said Sideplate, "and settle down and live there. If Sir Basil grows back to normal size, I shall let him stay on as my butler. If not, he can move into one of the houses on my model train set."

"Humph," said Sir Basil grumpily. (He was sitting on a matchbox on the table, nibbling at a peanut, which was the size of a roast turkey to him.) "If it hadn't been for you interfering pests, I'd have won the race and been the richest man in the world, not the tiniest."

"Oh, but inside, you were always a small man," said

the Snowfather. "You have just shrunk to fit yourself."

"The houses on my model train set are very nice," said Sideplate encouragingly. "You can settle down there, sir. And you'll certainly be the richest man in *that* world, so, in a way, you will have gotten your wish."

"Well, I'm going to settle down, too," said Helga Hammerfest, who had talked quietly and seriously with the Snowfather while the others were still eating. "I'm going to stay right here. That's my wish. It's the perfect place for polar bears, and for me, too. There was never enough winter in the world for my liking."

"What about you, Shen?" asked the Snowfather. "What's your wish?"

"I'm going to take all those diamonds back to Snowdovia and buy a fantastic new ship," said Shen. But now that he had the money to buy a ship, he felt a bit sad about it. He would be sorry to sail away from Sika. And when he looked at Sika he felt even sadder, because although she had a nice new snow-made hat and things, she hadn't come all this way for those—she had come so that the Snowfather could save her grandpa, and that was the one thing the Snowfather couldn't do.

After the feast they slept—a good night's sleep in white beds as deep and soft as snow-drifts. And when they woke, it was time to go home. Out in the Snowfather's garden, Sideplate was strapping Sir Basil's lunch box firmly to his sled, with Sir Basil buzzing inside it like a well-dressed wasp. Shackleton Jones was preparing his own sled for takeoff—he had fitted it with wings and propellers that he had made out of snow, and he was being helped by SNOBOT and by a new robot called SNOBOT 2, whom SNOBOT had made out of snow.

Helga was walking in the Snowfather's garden, watching her polar bears play on the

lawn. "This is the place for me," she said happily. "Ever since I was a little girl, I've wanted to come here, and to stay. No more dreary springs and summers for me. Winter is best. Winter *glitters*."

Shen and Sika went to where they had left Grandpa's sled. It was looking rather the worse for wear after its long journey. The leashes that tied the pugs to it were tattered and frayed.

"It's a long way for small paws," said the Snowfather, watching while they started arranging the little dogs.

That was true. The pugs did not look happy at the thought of the long journey that lay ahead. "But we have to go," said Sika. "It's lovely here, but we don't want to stay forever, like Helga." Then she looked at the Snowfather and said, "I've been thinking, about my wish . . ."

"You know I cannot give you your heart's desire," said the Snowfather.

"I know," she said. "But could you maybe give my grandpa *his* heart's desire instead?"

"And what would that be?"

"To see you, one more time," said Sika.

The Snowfather went quiet and thoughtful. While he was thinking, Shackleton Jones's sled went soaring overhead, with Shackleton and the SNOBOTs waving from the windows. It circled the igloo palace once and roared away into the south-southwest.

"That's the only way to travel," said the Snowfather approvingly, shading his eyes to watch the flying sled as it dwindled among the northern lights. He turned and ran back into his garden, to a fresh fall of anything-snow that had appeared overnight. Shen and Sika stood watching while he began shaping the snow into six big shapes. When he was finished, six huge elk shook themselves to life and started nibbling the grass while the Snowfather made six red harnesses for them and led them outside to where Shen and Sika's sled was waiting.

"Your dogs have run farther than any pugs ever ran before," he said as he started tying the elk to the sled. "It would be a pity to make them run all the way back again, too!"

There was barely enough room on the sled for Shen and Sika and the Snowfather and Shen's snow treasure chest and sixty-six pugs, but they all squeezed on somehow. When everyone was aboard, the Snowfather shouted something to his elk, and off they set, galloping across the snow with the sled rushing behind them, until the hiss of the sled's runners suddenly faded, and Shen looked over the side and saw that they were flying. The elk had unfolded great tawny wings and were flapping southward. The Snowfather's palace in its green ring of gardens was falling away below, with Helga Hammerfest waving,

and Sideplate looking up and waving, too, as he set out on his own journey.

Shen waved back, but pretty soon the sled was so high that he didn't think they could see him anymore. He could see them, though. He could see everything—the igloo palace and the abyss with its broken bridges and the fifty different kinds of snow. He could see, far away, the *Lost Hope* and, farther still, Kraken Deep and the dark forest, where the pugs' yipping had shaken down those clumps of snow. He could see all the wideness and whiteness of the frozen north, spread out under the northern lights like a map, or the iced top of a gigantic Christmas cake. And the Snowfather laughed and tugged on the elks' reins, and the sled flew south, toward the far-away, twinkling windows of Snowdovia.

FOURTEEN

It was midnight at the Po of Ice. On the big bed in the room behind the counter, Grandpa lay dreaming. His bed was a sled again, carrying him over the shining ice, under the glimmering green canopies of the northern lights.

Suddenly, he opened one eye. Was that wings he'd heard? Passing across the sky above the shop, settling on the snow outside . . .

Somewhere a door opened, quiet as quiet. A breath of cold stole into the warm room. The tiny sounds of tiptoed feet on floorboards.

Grandpa opened the other eye. "Oh, hello

there. I thought you were a dream," he said.

"I'm not," said the Snowfather, filling the room like a kindly shadow, stooping to fit his bigness under the slope of the ceiling.

"Then is my bed really a sled?" asked Grandpa. "Am I at the top of the world again?"

"No," said the Snowfather. "I have come south for a change. Helga Hammerfest and her bears will keep an eye on things at the Pole while I'm away. Sika tells me that you wanted to see me again."

"I wanted to come to you," said Grandpa. "I wanted to make that journey one last time. But I know I'm too old now for journeys. I will make do with the stories of Sika's journey instead."

"And I've got such stories to tell!" she said, and she climbed up onto the bed to put her arms around Grandpa's neck. "So many adventures, such things we've seen, me and Shen!"

And they started to tell him. The Snow-father stood listening, and after a while Sika's mom came in, woken by the voices. And there they all sat, the whole night long, while the northern lights shone in very brightly through the windows, and Grandpa and Sika and Shen and the Snowfather swapped their stories.

And toward morning, Grandpa fell asleep, still smiling at the memories of the things they'd told him. Deeper and deeper he sank into his dreams, and the sound of his snoring grew fainter and fainter, until at last it faded altogether, and they knew that he would not wake up.

They were sad and silent for a while, until the Snowfather said, "Come."

"Come where?" asked Sika's mother.

The Snowfather opened the door on the far side of Grandpa's bedroom. The cold came into the room. He went around behind Grandpa's bed and started to push it toward the open door. Shen and Sika ran to help—they did not know why he was pushing the bed outside, but they were sure he must have a good reason. After a moment, Sika's mom joined in, too. Together, the four of them eased the bed outside. It looked even more like a sled, standing there on the glittering snow.

The Snowfather stooped and scooped up a handful of the snow. He looked at it and smiled. "I thought so!" he said.

"What is it?" they asked.

"It is my favorite of all the fifty kinds of snow," he said.

He breathed on the clump of snow that was in his hand, and it came apart in soft white flakes. The flakes drifted into the air like loose feathers from a down comforter. It took Shen a moment to realize what was strange about them.